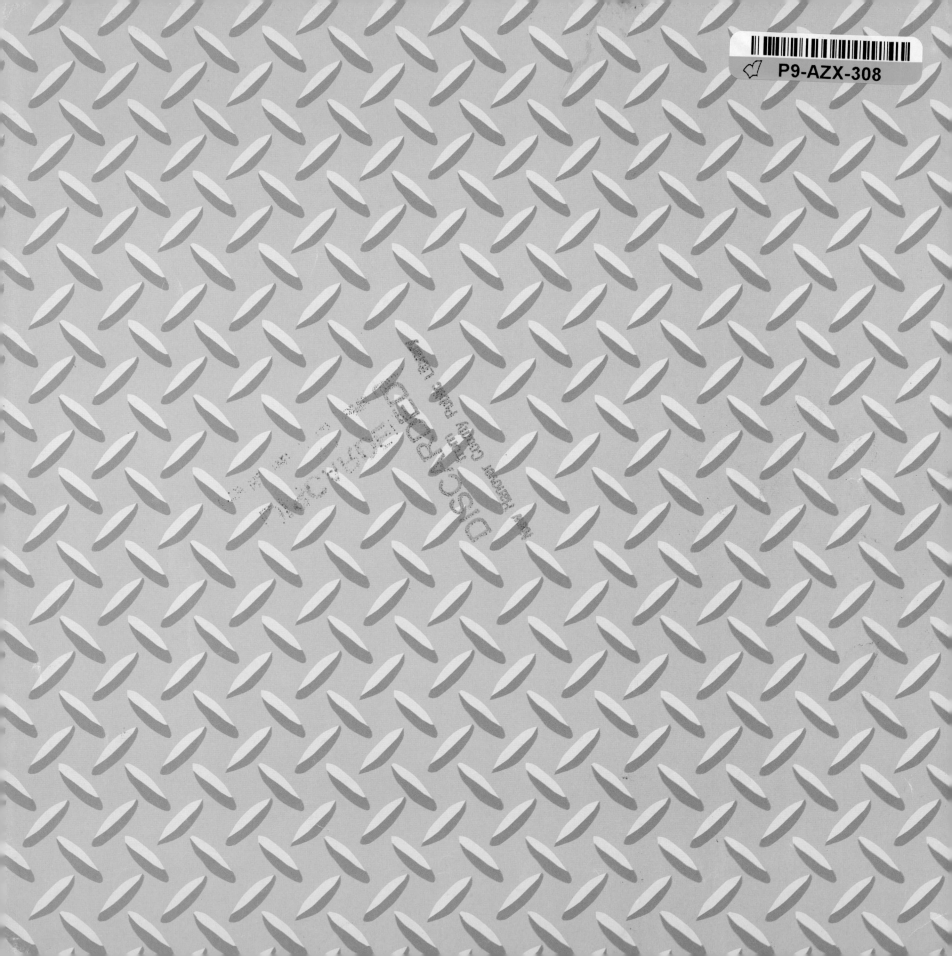

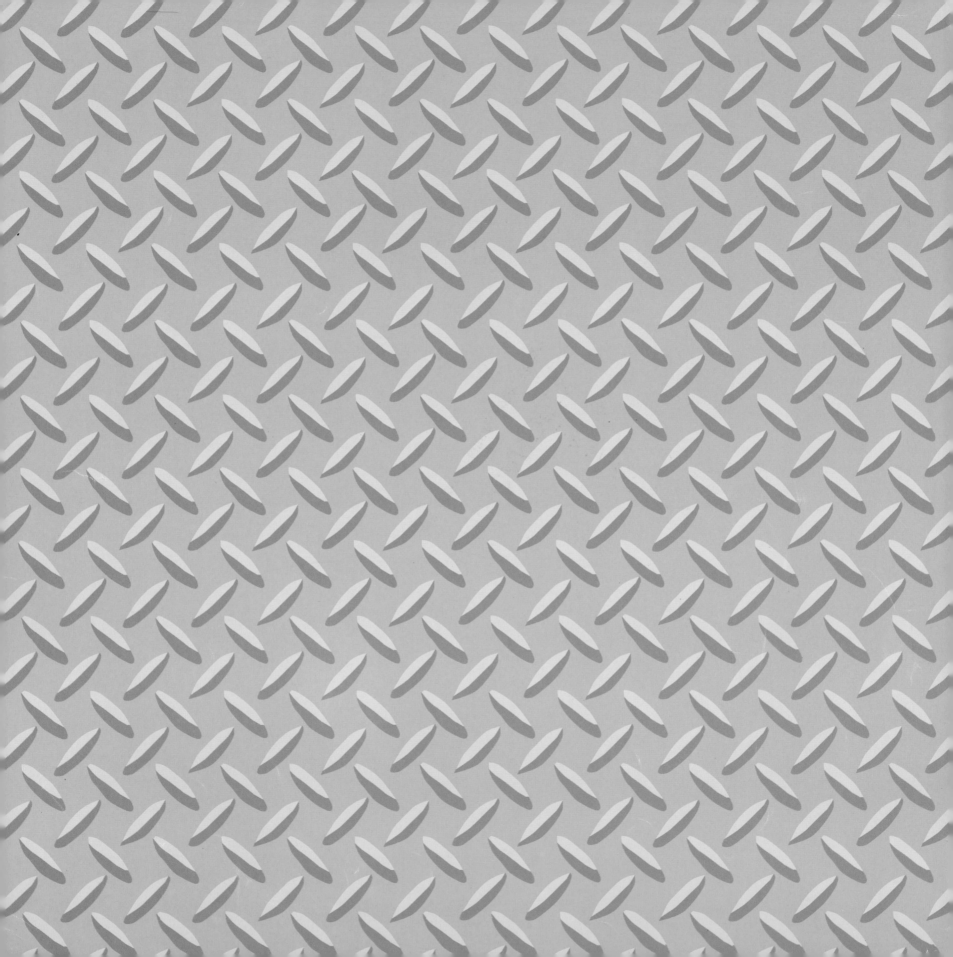

# Trucks Roll!

# Trucks Roll!

WORDS BY George Ella Lyon

ART BY Craig Frazier

A Richard Jackson Book

ATHENEUM BOOKS FOR YOUNG READERS

NEW YORK   LONDON   TORONTO   SYDNEY

Atheneum Books for Young Readers

An imprint of Simon & Schuster Children's Publishing Division

1230 Avenue of the Americas, New York, New York 10020

Book design by Craig Frazier

The text for this book is set in Serifa.

The illustrations for this book are rendered by hand and digitally colored.

Manufactured in China

First Edition

10 9 8 7 6 5 4 3 2 1

Library of Congress Cataloging-in-Publication Data

Lyon, George Ella, 1949–

Trucks roll! / George Ella Lyon ; illustrated by Craig Frazier.—1st ed.

p.   cm.

"A Richard Jackson book."

Summary: Illustrations and simple, rhyming text reveal many different—
and sometimes silly—items that trucks can haul.

ISBN-13: 978-1-4169-2435-7

ISBN-10: 1-4169-2435-3

[1. Stories in rhyme. 2. Trucks—Fiction. 3. Stories in rhyme.]  I. Frazier, Craig, 1955– ill. II. Title.

PZ8.3.L9893Tru 2007

[E]—dc22

2006010811

To Drew

*Go where the road and
the sky collide!*

     —Dad

To Sam and Jake Cohan;
Ace, Luke, and Leo Shelby;
and Ben Stoddard

*For the joy of the journey,
the wonder of the road!*

     —G. E. L.

Trucks' wheels
go 'round and 'round.
Trucks' pistons
go up and down.

Trucks roll!

Trucks have trailers.
Trucks have cabs.
Some haul rabbits.
Some haul labs.

Some haul apple juice.
Some haul trees.
Water them down
in the desert, please.

Trucks roll!

Trucks bring ice cream.
Trucks bring blocks,
books and bulldozers,
dolls and clocks.

Dispatcher calls,
says Get underway!
Chocolate chip cookies
have to travel today.

Stacks of puzzles
ready to load.
Spaceships, toy trains—
get them on the road!

Haul them through mountains,
over rivers, past towns—
around blue sky curves,
through rain pouring down.

Trucks roll!

Steering wheel, radio,
horn's deep beep.
TV in the bunk
where tired truckers sleep.

Trucks stop.

Stop for traffic lights.
Stop for tolls.
Stop for pork chops
and cinnamon rolls.

Stop for weigh stations.
Stop for gas.
Stop for the night
to let sleepiness pass.

Stars above like headlight beams:
truckers travel rolling dreams.

Then, key in the slot,
coffee in the cup,
trucker's at the wheel
when the sun comes up.

Trucks roll!

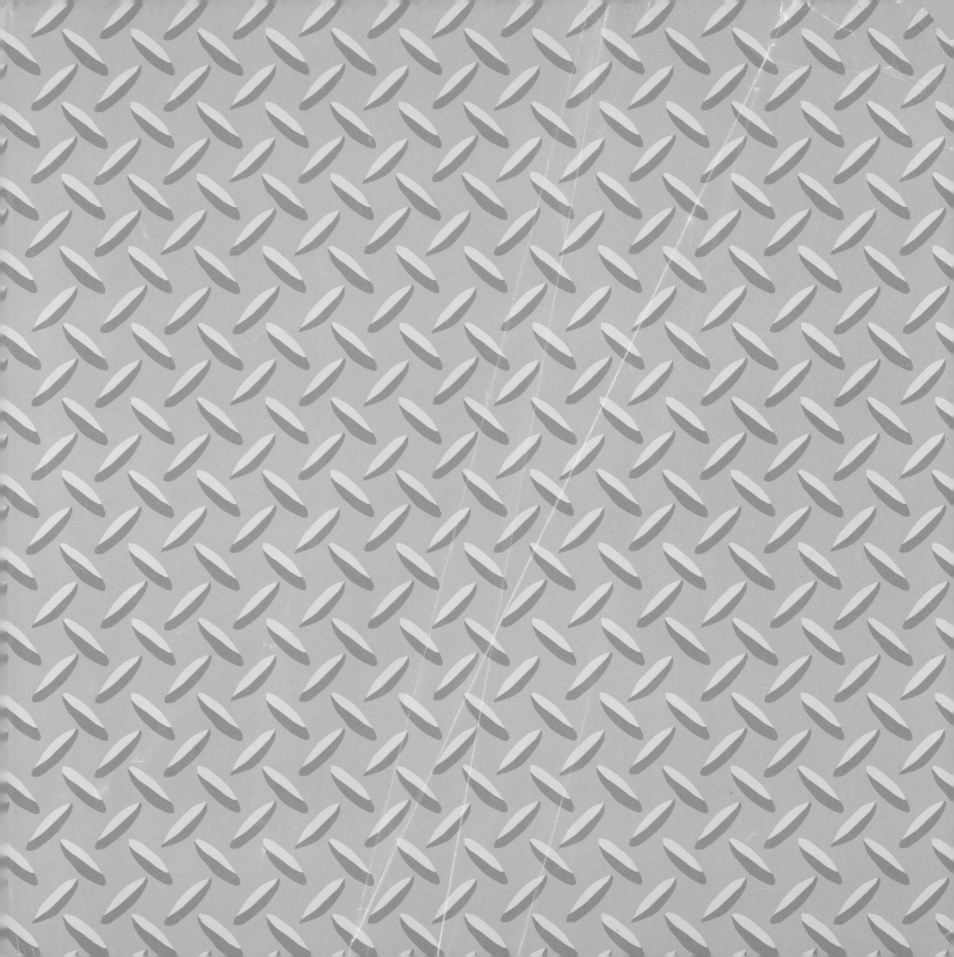

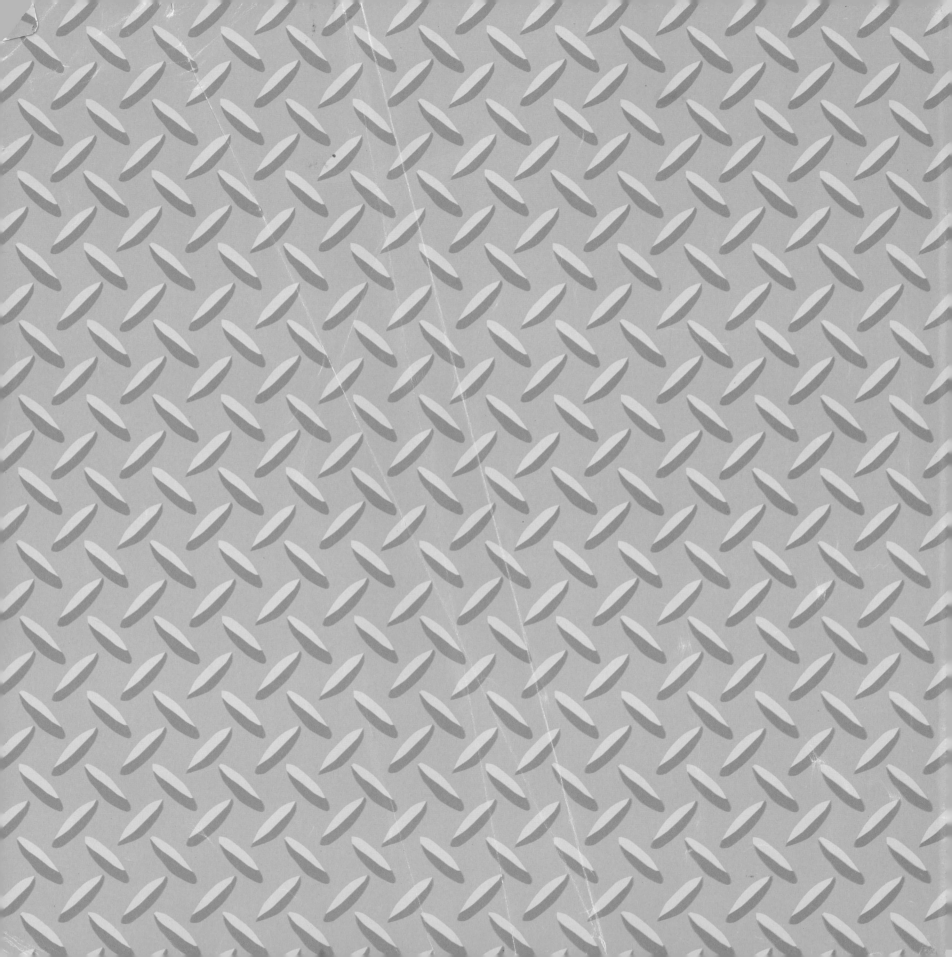